U0022232

For Gemk,

Whose endless supply of ideas and honest critique made this possible.

感謝 Gemk

源源不絕的靈感及誠懇的建議讓這一切成真。

The Brain
大頭比利

Coleen Reddy 著

曹武亦 繪

薛慧儀 譯

三民書局

Billy is a really smart boy. He knows everything.
He knows more than his friends,
his parents and his teachers.

比利是個非常聰明的男孩。
他什麼事都知道。
他知道的東西，比爸爸媽媽、
老師、還有他的朋友都要多。

3

Because Billy is so smart, people call him "BRAIN."
His brain is so big that his head is twice as big as his body.
He looks strange with his big head.

因為比利太聰明了，所以大家都叫他「金頭腦」。
他的腦好大，大到他的頭足足有他身體的兩倍呢！
頂著這麼一顆大頭，看起來真的很奇怪。

5

Billy reads books every day.
The more he reads, the bigger his brain gets.
The bigger his brain gets, the bigger his head gets.

比利每天都看書。
書讀得愈多，腦袋裡的東西就愈多。
腦袋裝得愈多，他的頭也就變得更大了。

One day, Billy reads and reads and reads.
His head grows so big that he cannot leave his house.
His big head cannot fit through the door.

有一天，比利不停地讀呀讀，
結果他的頭長得太大，讓他根本沒辦法離開家裡。
他的頭已經大得連門都擠不出去了！

Billy's parents are so sad.

They do not know what to do.

The house is breaking because Billy's head is growing.

比利的爸媽好著急，
他們不知道該怎麼辦。
比利的頭還在繼續長大，
眼看著房子就快被撐破了。

Everyone comes to look at Billy's big brain.
They stand outside waiting for the house to fall down.
Someone says, "You should ask Billy what to do.
He is so smart. He will know."

所有人都來看比利的大頭。
他們站在屋外，等著看房子垮下來。
有人說：「應該去問問比利啊！
他這麼聰明，一定知道該怎麼辦。」

So Billy's parents ask him, "Son, our house is going to break
because your brain is so big. What can we do?"
Billy screams from inside the house, "Every time I read,
I get smarter and my brain gets bigger.
I must do something that will make me
stupid and my brain will get smaller."

於是爸媽就問了：「兒子啊，我們的房子就快被你的大頭撐垮了。
我們該怎麼辦呢？」
比利在屋裡大聲喊著：「我每次讀書，都會變得更聰明，
頭也就更大。我一定得想辦法變笨，這樣我的頭就會變小了。」

15

"What makes people stupid?" ask his parents.
Everybody thinks and thinks.
"I know, I know," says a voice.

I KNOW,
I KNOW,

「什麼東西會使人變笨呢?」他的爸媽問。
每個人都努力地想啊想。
「我知道,我知道。」有個聲音說。

18

It is a little boy.
He says, "I know what makes people stupid.
My mother always says that watching too much television
will make me stupid. Maybe it will make Billy
stupid and his head will get smaller."

原來是一個小男孩。
他說：「我知道什麼可以讓人變笨。我媽媽總是說，
看太多電視會讓我變笨。也許看電視會讓比利變笨，
他的頭就會小一點了。」

"Yes, yes," say all the children.
"We can try it," say Billy's parents.
They get a big satellite dish.
There are 100 channels for Billy to watch.

「對呀！對呀！」所有的小孩也一起附和。

「那我們就來試試看吧！」比利的爸爸媽媽說。

他們找來一個很大的衛星小耳朵，讓比利可以看一百個電視頻道。

They tell Billy to watch television.
Billy watches television and stops reading.
After a while, everyone hears lots of laughter.

他們要比利看電視。
於是比利停止讀書，開始看電視。
過了一會兒，大家聽到一陣陣的笑聲。

It is Billy.

He is laughing so much that he starts to cry.

"More, more! I want more!" he screams.

是比利在笑呢！

他笑得太用力，以致於眼淚都流出來了。

「再多一點！再多一點！我要看更多的電視節目！」他大叫著。

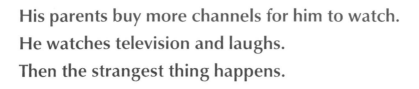

His parents buy more channels for him to watch.
He watches television and laughs.
Then the strangest thing happens.

於是他的爸媽就買了更多的頻道讓他看。
他一邊看著電視，一邊笑個不停。
然後，最奇怪的事情發生了！

Billy's head really does get smaller.
Little by little, it shrinks.
After some time, his head is normal.

比利的頭真的變小了耶！
一點一點地，他的頭開始縮小了。
過沒多久，他的頭就恢復到正常大小了。

But Billy cannot stop watching television.
His head is getting smaller.
"Oh no!" says his mother. "Now his head will be too small."

但比利卻沒辦法停止看電視。
於是他的頭愈縮越小，愈縮越小……
「哎呀！糟了！」他的媽媽說，
「現在他的頭又太小了。」

Billy's parents take the television away from him before his brain gets too small.

"Son," says his father. "You should not read too much or watch too much television. You should go out and play some sport."
"Okay," says Billy.

比利的爸媽趕緊把電視搬走，免得他的頭變得太小。

「兒子呀，」他的爸爸說：「你不應該讀太多書或是看太多電視，你應該到外頭走走，做點兒運動。」
「好吧！」比利說。

33

Billy wants to play soccer.
But now that his brain isn't big,
he cannot remember how to play soccer.
He decides to go to his room and read about soccer.
"Oh dear," says his mom. "Here we go again."

比利想要去踢足球。
可是他腦子裡的東西已經沒剩多少,所以他想不起來該怎麼踢足球了。
他決定回房裏讀讀關於足球的書。
「喔!天哪!」他的媽媽說。「又來了!」

讓我們來做書籤

你是不是像大頭比利一樣愛看書呢？如果是的話，你千萬不可以錯過這個好機會，學習做一個屬於你自己的書籤喔！

 工具與材料

1. 舊的信封　　3. 彩色筆
2. 剪刀　　　　4. 膠帶

* 在做勞作之前，要記得在桌上先鋪一張紙或墊板，才不會把桌面弄得髒兮兮喔！

步驟

1. 將舊信封的一角剪下來。
2. 用彩色筆裝飾剪下來的三角形。
3. 裝飾好後，再用膠帶黏在邊緣的部分，可以讓書籤的壽命更長久喔！

生字表

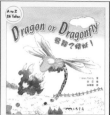

A to Z
26 Tales

二十六個妙朋友，陪你一起

愛閱雙語叢書

✿26個妙朋友系列✿

二十六個英文字母，二十六冊有趣的讀本，最適合初學英文的你！

快樂學英文！

精心錄製的雙語CD，
　　讓孩子學會正確的英文發音
用心構思的故事情節，
　　讓兒童熟悉生活中常見的單字
特別設計的親子活動，
　　讓家長和小朋友一起動動手、動動腦

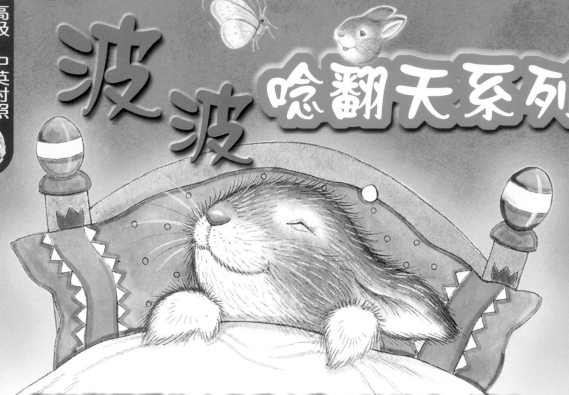

國家圖書館出版品預行編目資料

The Brain:大頭比利 / Coleen Reddy著；曹武亦繪；
　薛慧儀譯.－－初版一刷.－－臺北市；三民，
2003
　　面；　公分－－(愛閱雙語叢書.二十六個妙朋
　友系列) 中英對照
　ISBN 957－14－3777－8　 (精裝)

　1.英國語言－讀本

523.38　　　　　　　　　　　　　　92008798

ⓒ　The Brain
—— 大頭比利

著作人　Coleen Reddy
繪　圖　曹武亦
譯　者　薛慧儀
發行人　劉振強
著作財
產權人　三民書局股份有限公司
　　　　臺北市復興北路386號
發行所　三民書局股份有限公司
　　　　地址／臺北市復興北路386號
　　　　電話／(02)25006600
　　　　郵撥／0009998－5
印刷所　三民書局股份有限公司
門市部　復北店／臺北市復興北路386號
　　　　重南店／臺北市重慶南路一段61號
初版一刷　2003年7月
　編　號　S 85635－1
　定　價　新臺幣壹佰捌拾元整
行政院新聞局登記證局版臺業字第○二○○號

ISBN　957－14－3777－8　 (精裝)